I Have a Brother

by Smiljana Čoh

tiger tales

This is my brother.

He is very small.

I am
much
bigger.

My brother
is happy to
have me

because I make him laugh.

I show him what
big brothers can do.

I can kick a ball,

jump,

run,

and ride my bike.

My brother loves to
sleep on Daddy's chest.

When I was small, I loved
to sleep in Mommy's arms.

Now I can sleep
in my big bed.

My brother wears diapers.

When I was small,
I wore diapers too.

Now I can use the toilet . . .

with a little help.

My brother is happy most of the time, but sometimes he cries. So I sing to him.

When he gets bigger,
I will let him use
my bicycle . . .

because he's my brother
and I love him sooo much!

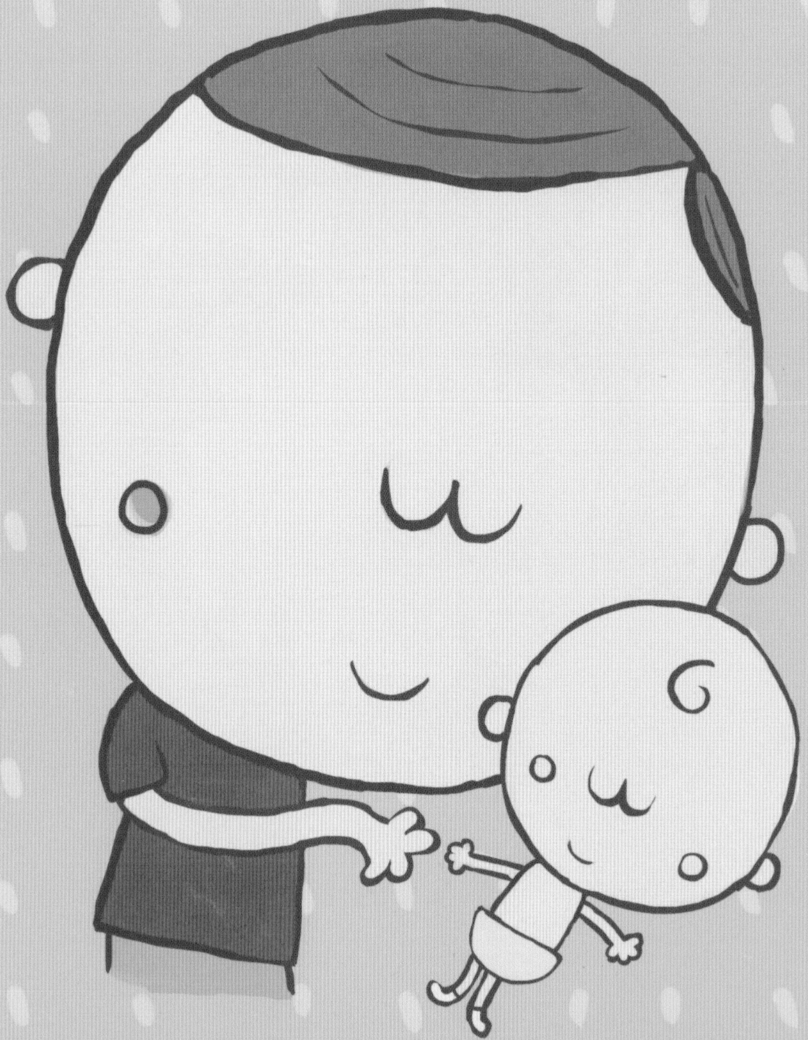